Alice Modern

Alice Modern

a novel

Michelle Auerbach

XOXOX
PRESS
Gambier, Ohio

Alice Modern – a novel

copyright © 2016 Michelle Auerbach

ISBN 978-1-880977-44-6

Book design by Jerry Kelly

Editorial assistance by Kaitlin Tebeau

Cover painting by Anna Muntada Torrelas

Excerpts from H.D. and Bryher letters from
Analyzing Freud, edited by Susan Stanford Friedman,
New Directions, November 2002

Published by XOXOXpress, Gambier OH 43022

Printed & distributed by IngramSpark worldwide

Available at ingram.com, amazon.com & xoxoxpress.com

Library of Congress CIP Cataloguing in Publication Data

Names: Auerbach, Michelle, 1968- author.
Title: Alice Modern : a novel / by Michelle Auerbach.
Description: Gambier, OH : XOXOXpress, 2016.
Identifiers: LCCN 2016020702 | ISBN 9781880977446
Subjects: LCSH: H. D. (Hilda Doolittle), 1886-1961--Friends and
  associates--Fiction. | Women authors--Fiction. | Modernism
  (Literature)--Fiction. | Americans--Austria--Fiction. |
  Austria--History--1918-1938--Fiction. | Vienna (Austria)--History--20th
  century--Fiction. | GSAFD: Biographical fiction.
Classification: LCC PS3601.U3478 A79 2016 | DDC 813/.6--dc23
LC record available at https://lccn.loc.gov/2016020702

"Wo Es war, soll Ich werden."
Where it was, I am to become.
SIGMUND FREUD

Preface

There was a time in my life when I was young and inexperienced enough not to know what suffering can do to the human psyche. I believed what Nietzsche said: whatever does not kill you makes you stronger. This was when my only experience came from books and the lives of the people who wrote them. I did not yet know that suffering can distort the soul into a hideous scarred little thing, scared of the daylight, a twisted repository of fears and angers accessible only in the way the mind skitters away from a subject. The way, for instance, an advertisement in the newspaper for a bank can make a person quickly turn the page. He does not know why he is disturbed, only that he cannot stand the sight of that particular advertisement. The unappeasable, angry, bruised, and scalded lump of hair and bile that is his soul sees the eagle on the bank's crest and it makes him feel in some small, quick way what he felt standing on the Heldenplatz, in the shadow of Prince Eugene's horse, holding his father's hand and listening to the crowd roar when Hitler spoke. He saw the twitch as his father's jaw tightened. Now, he could as easily explain the connection between needing to turn the page and Hitler as tell you the price of a loaf of bread in Naples. While we savor our pleasant memories consciously, roll them around in the mind like a caramel on the tongue as the sugar melts off, we hold our suffering deeper. It is not our pleasant memories that leave us averse to eagles and perversely attached to something else, something darker and more insistent. Our pleasant memories remain explicable. I love the scent of linden trees because their fragrance reminds me of the park I played in with my sister when we were small. I love the pastry shop on Kensington High Street because they make the thinnest strudel I have tasted since the days when my brother would sneak me a plate when my parents had guests and I, younger, was forced to bed. These attractions, and their concomitant memories, I can explain. The rest, I may not even be aware of.

I once believed that whatever scrapes I found myself in and whatever difficulties I encountered would mold me into a glamorous, dangerous, and experienced woman. A convenient fantasy while I was still mostly a child and had not yet had any hair-raising encounters with the side of people that allows them to perpetrate violence and aggression on a scale humans were never meant to fathom. I believed, from knowing a woman who survived such violence during the Great War, that her laconic, alluring distance was caused by her pain, and that if I ever experienced anything of any import, I would myself become appealing and mysterious. I wanted nothing more than to suffer a bit, so that I could metamorphose into the woman I felt I deserved to be. That woman would be sensitive, magnetic, brilliant, reclusive, hedonistic, beautiful, mysterious, intelligent, free, and kind. In my youth and innocence, I hoped a good dose of real life could change me into this ideal: it never crossed my mind that it might simply distort me.

It did not happen as I had hoped when I was younger. Suffering came, of course, as it does to every lifetime. That hardship scarred me, it transformed me, and yet, I did not become like anyone else. My suffering did not strengthen into the magnetism I craved, but instead I grew frayed – still recognizable as the same Alice Modern I was in my youth. I was still me.

At some point, you become old enough to understand a story well enough to tell it. This means you have the experience to know which parts are important and which can be subsumed in the general hubbub of life, not missed, not important. Too little distance and you may not place the correct importance on the correct elements. You may value too highly the parts that make you see yourself the way you would like, and not stress the moments when you collided with a person or an historic event that would later become inextricably bound to your story. It is my opinion that you have to grow into an understanding, earn it. This is not based on cleverness or attitude, beauty or luck. The ability to tell a story correctly is pure perseverance.

My story, the story of Alice Modern, begins in earnest the day I was hired by a poet-lady and her dearest friend to come to Vevey, in Switzerland, to be the nanny to her daughter, Perdita. I lived a while before that, and as I have said, there was strudel and there were linden trees with their sickly sweet scent. There was Vienna, there was music, and there were always books. There was no real story. The day I met Kat and Gryphon, as they called each other, that was the point where I could begin to draw the trajectory of my life. I owe to those two women, and to baby Perdita, who would grow to be a sweet young woman, my continued existence on this harsh and beautiful plane as they rescued me first from bourgeois Vienna and my claustrophobic family, then from myself, and finally from Adolph Hitler. There is no way to repay the favor except to tell what I know of them and how they intersect with my story as carefully and truthfully as I possibly can.

Chapter 1

All I think about is Victor. Nothing, absolutely nothing, distracts me from wondering when I will see him again. He is, every minute, on my mind. Not just the way I first saw him at the pool at the Stadion- bad, in his swimming trunks, standing on a platform, arms raised above his head ready to dive into the water, focused on the other side of the river. I knew by how graceful he was – more so than anyone around him – that he was about to win a swim contest. I think about how he looks in his glasses, sitting at a café table reading the newspaper, or how his voice sounds when he speaks. He says certain words, the word "so," and he uses it often, and it reminds me of that way poets speak, the very fancy ones in Switzerland. I follow my thoughts as they skip between the crocuses in the sidewalk cracks to my boot tip to the edges of his green woolen jacket to the whispers of war to his cheekbones to the air that stings my nostrils when I pull it into my nose.

I wish I could hold him in my mind long enough to touch him, bold as that is, or to talk to him, or to stare at him when he is not looking. But he moves around so much. Sometimes he is a voice, sometimes the smell of cigarettes outside on a cold morning. Sometimes he is the body with beads of water running off.

When I stared too much that first day by the pool, Lucie mocked me.

"Alice wants to take his trunks off."

"Lucie, don't be crude."

"That's how you're looking at him."

"I wouldn't know."

She looked at me for a moment, her perfect pointed chin tilted to one side, her brown eyes bunched up at the edges.

"Alice, you're twenty-one, have you never been with a man before?"

"Of course not," I said, sounding too much like my older sister Klara for my taste.

"Oh, my," Lucie said, her hand over her mouth. She leaned in close to me and said slowly and quietly as if she thought I was stupid, and not just prudish, "Alice Modern, you are wasting your life."

A day or two goes by in which I have not seen Victor and, finally, I become aware that hours have passed and I have not imagined how I can get close enough to touch him. I am at the Opera with my sister, or with Dr. Jekels on the couch staring at his ceiling trying to find things to say to keep him interested in my analysis, or talking with Kat, who has come to Vienna to be a patient of Dr. Freud, and in those moments, my skin no longer pulls toward him, no longer stings. I notice it first as a lack. I miss the tingle on the surface of my skin that I feel when I think of him, exactly as if he were holding his fingers just above my skin, making the hairs stand on end.

Not that I ever do touch him. Nor could I ever touch him. I cannot say I have ever spoken to him directly. But, I sit by him in the Café Central, and I read the papers he puts back on the desk by the window, and I have thought about taking a cigarette he put out, and touching it to my lips.

Still, when I went to the Café Central with Lucie, I sat just outside his circle and listened to what he said, and I knew his thoughts on everything from sport to why Latin has so many words for pork. I saw him glance at us girls, and smile. Lucie, with her athlete's confidence and wide-lipped smile that makes her think everyone wants her, can talk to him.

"Alice, how will you ever get him alone if you can't even speak to him? I see him looking at you, all you have to do is look him in the eye and smile. That's what men need, the smallest taste of encouragement."

"He's too perfect. I can't. I will look like an idiot. And besides, no one does that here. Vienna is not Paris, or Vevey, after all."

"Who cares, mousy Alice, he doesn't even know anyone you know. He'll never meet your parents or show up at someone's house for coffee after dinner. He can be our secret."

"Right," I tell her, trying to sound worldly like Kat, "Our secret *goyische* lover."

I didn't look back at his table. My cheeks were too hot and I knew they would tell everyone who saw me the tales of desire Lucie was spinning into the air.

That he's Christian isn't even the problem. He has not lived with Kat and Dawg, Gryphon and Pup. He has not left Vienna.

Most people stay here forever until they die, so proud of their fair city and their culture. Why go anywhere else? Everything and every-one and anything and anyone worth any amount are right here. My mother certainly has no idea Vienna is provincial, or that we Jews brought all the culture here with us from other places anyway. I have been fortunate. I did leave, lived somewhere else – worked, even if it was as a nanny – and I am not the same person as I was before I lived in Villa Kenwin. Though, when I walk at night through my family's apartment, touching the roses carved in the wood on the backs of the chairs, I can-not believe a house like Kenwin exists. The moment I came back it was as if the river closed above my head and the world of Villa Kenwin never even happened. The same world that houses my mother's flower-sprigged china and the atmosphere it creates of self-satisfaction and cheerful smugness, could not possibly also hold the clean square lines of Kenwin, which brook no ornamenta-tion.

I was there, in Vevey. I lived in that house, walked on the balconies late at night after Pup fell asleep, touched the straight, cold metal railings. I have seen the outline of that house in the moonlight and in the sun, and I know that plain, rectangular box of a house holds complexities. Kenwin holds intricacies all these rosettes and embroidered cloths I crocheted myself but a few years ago, lying abject on end tables in my family sitting room, cannot imagine. Nor can anyone who lives here. Including me. That fact, that simple fact − I was at Kenwin, now I am here − is making me slowly go mad.

Victor is small inside, encumbered by the aspirations warring within him to be his father and to fight what comes to us from the North. At Kenwin I learned to expand inside, to find the edges of myself and to laugh at them.

I want to touch him. I am frightening in my desires. When I lived at Villa Kenwin, I saw Kat and Gryphon fill their house with desires: books, friends, food, wine, and sometimes the silence of both of them at their typewriters contemplating the world. They wrote books with desire, they gardened with desire, they filled each and every movement they made on any day from the fountain of their desires.

They are writers, artists; they had permission to live like that. Creating poems and novels gives you reason to live however you want. Gives you an obligation to largeness and exploration. My world in Vienna is filled only with what fits neatly in the head. Because it cannot coexist with family and ideals and morals and my mother's china, desire is uncanny here. It is forbidden. Worse, it is pushed down, down, down out of the sight of the good people of the city.

There are people who are allowed to live exactly as they want, and then there are people like me, here, who are not. It is as simple as the difference in the houses. One house is sleek, but the people are complex because there the inside of people is what matters, not the perfect appearance. Not that beauty does not count. It does. In that world beauty radiates. In Vienna, beauty counts only on the exterior of things, people, ideas. Beauty is not to be explored, touched, tasted, and definitely not made love to.

"Straighten that rug Alice, you don't want people to think you don't know how to keep a house, you'll never get married that way," my mother scolds.

"Someone teach poor Alice to sew better, she has to at least look well trained."

"Alice, you play the piano beautifully, read Goethe and Schiller, and still you manage to embarrass us."

At Villa Kenwin, I tried and tried to grasp how I was supposed to live so that when the time came to leave, I would be able to be like Kat and mostly like Gryphon, but sometimes I think I only left with facts about them stored: Kat's Americanisms and her long correspondence with this or that magazine and this or that poet, and Gryphon's stories about traveling down the Nile in a boat as a child and exploring pyramids. Dr. Jekels says they are deep in my unconscious. I would agree, and add that they are deep in my heart. But that does not give me the directions that would allow me to be any different. I have been so well trained on the outsides of things that I would need so much longer to absorb how to live if I were going to live myself from the inside out.

Chapter 2

r. Jekels says "Hmmm." I knew he would say that. Kat warned me. I try to summarize, saying, "Once, I was a girl in Vienna living with my sister Klara, my brother Ernst, and my mother in our flat, and I was, if not happy, then busy. I was an automaton. I rushed from school to home to the houses of my friends, or from home to the bookstore where my sister works. I read and played the piano, sewed, and helped my mother whenever I could stand to hear her prattling on about who married whom and which girls looked good in which dresses. At school, I had friends who, like Lucie, were mostly the daughters of other Jewish families dressed in pretty clothes and filled with an honest regard for the intellect. We talked about philosophy, and Goethe's poem in which the moth flies into the flame of desire and experience, and how we hoped that intensity would happen to us some day. Tell a wise man or else stay silent, Goethe says. Good advice. Talking to the daughters of the Viennese bureaucrats who also went to our school was like playing nursemaid. Their copybooks were immaculate, but their minds were too compliant. They were children; we were the outsiders who saw things and felt things much more deeply."

He nods. This is what Kat said he would do, so I keep talking.

"I never thought about my parents as a child, you know. Men and women. Love."

"Hmm."

"Sex?"

"Hmm," he says, and this time he nods.

I stare off into space.

"I am in love."

He says "Hmmm" with more vigor. I cannot follow through. I slide sideways into another topic.

"I was asked to come to Vevey, Switzerland from Vienna by two ladies named Hilda Doolittle and Winifred Ellerman to be nanny to their daughter."

He does not respond at all.

"They are the ones paying you for my analysis. You know them, and you know they are worried about me. The change between their life and this one is so extreme. They are worried. Miss Ellerman jokes, 'We broke Alice.'"

I explain this to introduce my feelings about Victor, because they are so tied to that other life. He nods. No noise. I have lost the trail. Not yet ready to tell all about my feelings and not sure where to proceed.

"May I call them by their nicknames? It is what I am used to."

He stares at me looking like a kindly jaguar. Kat told me the story of the jaguar god of the underworld and the sky god working together to make the sun go round through the dark and the heavens every day. She knows all those myths, especially the Greek ones. She talks of Artemis as though they were in school together back in Pennsylvania, in America, and Artemis will be visiting soon. Dr. Jekels looks like the jaguar she described, with his round glasses with round eyes inside, and his big ears. Perhaps if I threw some burning incense into the lake, he would be appeased.

I tell him the simple facts of the story. Kat lay in a bedsit in London after the war and

Gryphon found her. Gryphon says she found the one person she could have a lifetime's conversation with and never, never grow bored or feel restless. They shared that most important connection of books and ideas.

Gryphon visited Kat in that tiny apartment for the first time on a winter's day after the end of the Great War. They both survived, but as Gryphon says, getting over the war was harder than living through it. Gryphon came to call without even knowing Kat, having only corresponded passionately about books and poems until Kat felt comfortable enough to invite her to tea. Gryphon saw that Kat would die. Kat was so ill and the war so recently over, and Gryphon had seen a lot of death. Kat felt it too, that she'd survived the bombing but was going to have to give in now. They talked for hours, and the sun, weak as it was, began to disappear from the window. With it, all the color faded from Kat's face.

"You've described Greece to me," Kat told Gryphon, "and now I am afraid I won't live to see it."

This terrified Gryphon, who would do anything for Kat, even though they'd known each other only a few hours.

"If you live, and you will, I will take you to Greece this summer, and every summer until you can't stand one more pillar or statue of Athena," Gryphon told her, and she meant it, even though it sounded impossible after the war and with how ill Kat looked at that moment.

Kat's cheeks were pale and in all the crevices of her face there were grey lines and shadows. She was too thin to be eight months pregnant and her nightgown was too big, even at the shoulder. Kat had no food in the room, and no one to bring her any. The landlady was afraid to catch influenza, another tenant was dying, and Kat was alone on the top floor with no food, a cold hearth, and Pup growing inside her. Gryphon – and I can just see her because she is so intimidating – stood up to the landlady.

In her most imperious voice she said, "Miss Doolittle will have a fire, and someone to keep it burning, and she will have soup, and will not be left alone for a moment until I come back." Then Gryphon looked down at the landlady to let her know that no one ever crossed her.

Gryphon, while not so tall, looks vaguely like a French bulldog, making people hop to. It must be her mind, because when she gives an order, and she seldom does, no one ever questions her.

When Gryphon tells the story, she says that her upbringing to be a good girl, so much like mine, made her rush home to her parents. They would not allow a girl to stay out past six in the evening. The whole time she was at home she felt queasy. How could she leave Kat, who she'd only just found, and risk losing her? How could she neglect the woman who in those few hours became her every thought? But, she had set Kat's recovery into motion with her commands. That was enough. That changed the world.

For Gryphon, Kat started out as a poem in an anthology of Imagist poetry, which Gryphon will take out and show you. The slim volume is bound in blue cloth, the edges of the paper hand cut. Gryphon will tell you, "This is how I found her." That day, Kat became Gryphon's life.

She found Kat a nurse and made sure Kat lived. Gryphon's will took over and Kat had to acquiesce. It would be lovely to feel that powerful. How I long to mold the world like Gryphon.

Gryphon is married. So is Kat. They are respectable ladies. Gryphon married Dawg, a man who loves boys. Kenneth MacPherson is Dawg's name. Dawg offered to marry Gryphon so that she could live her own life away from her parents, and so that he could have the money to live in Paris and cavort with whomever he chose. Now she and Kat are two nice married ladies sharing a house with one husband, Dawg, who sometimes stops by. Except that Dawg's boys wander through, each blacker and younger than the last. They trip so lightly up the stairs and the noises that waft back down make me wonder how come they don't stay forever. I would if someone made those noises exude from me. There are also Kat's lovers, and Gryphon's potential lovers. This year, I hear it is Elisabeth Bergner, the actress, who comes to bat her eyes at Gryphon.

You might wonder about Kat's husband. We do not mention him, except to use his name as a swear word. Cuthbert, Kat's legal husband, left her pregnant for some other woman during the war, but Kat never divorced him. Cuthbert's name has become a swear word around Kenwin.

A Cuthbert is a coward and a back-stabber.

I forgot I was talking to Dr. Jekels, and when I look around, I realize I am on his red crushed velvet fainting couch, staring at a wall of leather-spined books filled with a longing to smell them and touch them. They glow like jewels or a stained glass window in a dusty Italian church. They mock my memories of other people's love. We books tell the truth. You, Alice, you lie by omission.

"Thank you Miss Modern," Dr. Jekels says. At once, I am out of the room, the building, and alone again with my thoughts. I will try harder next time to talk about myself. It lingers, the feeling of Kenwin, like smoke in my hair. Luxurious smoke, rich cigar smoke, but soft, transferred to my pillow as I sleep.

Chapter 3

I must fix the part of me that has learned to be like Gryphon, because at home I cannot want so much so strongly. When Gryphon wants something – an idea, a book, a trip, a person – she draws the object of her desire magnetically. Her want is so huge and childlike that we all want it for her too.

Lucie and I sit outside the Dianabad, where her sports club Hakoach practices, and we formulate a plan. Boys and girls walk in with fencing clothes draped over their shoulders, like a second set of pale skin kept just in case. Swimmers saunter by, hair wet from the pool, looking tired. Each person stops to say hello or good-bye and Lucie smiles at everyone. She knows more people in this building than I know in the whole city. Lucie wants to get started right away.

"Alice, don't you feel it? There is no time to lose!"

"But, Lucie, I just *can't*. It's a dense fog, this

feeling, and I can't think my way through it."

"Of course not, you silly little girl. This is not a moment for thinking. This is a moment for Alice Modern's desire to let loose on Vienna."

She doesn't hear any of the details I have gleaned about Victor, that he is studying law, what he thinks about Loos and Klimt; she just wants action.

"We will go to the coffeehouse and wait for Victor, you silly girl. I will talk to him first since I can see by how red your ears are that you will muck it up."

"Lucie, I have desire, maybe too much desire."

"No such thing as too much desire, gorgeous. You just come over once we are talking and I will introduce you."

"But what if I aim all this desire at Victor and he does not swoon at my feet in eternal gratitude? What if he laughs at me, or hisses something horrible, you know? This feeling, here, this is not what I was raised to do."

"Oh, Alice, I am so sorry. There is nothing unusual about how you feel, except that you think about it too much. Let's go before you lose your nerve."

"But, what if he does not appreciate me?"

"Men, you gorgeous little bit of fluff, are very appreciative when your clothes come off, without fail, and every time."

She is right. I have seen as much at Kenwin. No matter who is leading whom into a room and pulling the door shut, at that moment, their eyes are unfocused and their skin flushed. Like mine now. So I walk in silence, hoping for the best.

Our shoes make a staccato rhythm. Mine, with less heel, make a lower sound and Lucie's, with a buckle on the front, sound jingly and sharp. My coat flaps open and shut, sometimes covering my knees and sometimes leaving them exposed, and the sky is the dark blue of a satin gown on the way to evening. I want to take the streetcar.

"No, little chicken," She says, "you are so pretty when your cheeks are rosy from the air, eyes damp from the wind. Your black hair and pale skin make a perfect setting for those inviting blue eyes."

"Be careful, Lucie," I try to joke to dispel my nerves, "that phrase sounds familiar. Isn't that what Hitler says Vienna needs, the proper setting for the pearl?"

She stops walking and turns slowly around and slaps me, harder than a joke, but she doesn't give it her all or she would knock me down. I will not start to cry.

"It isn't funny, Alice."

"I know it's not, but if you can't laugh at it..."

But she has lost her sense of humor.

I want to tell her that if you can't laugh at it, you're dead, but she is gone, five steps ahead of me and I can tell she is crying by her coat moving up on her shoulders. I didn't do anything wrong, I tell myself over and over till I work up a righteous indignation. At Kenwin, we don't shrink from the news, we bring it right out into the open. I follow her around the corner and wonder if she will walk right past the door, but she pulls it open hard and lets it bang shut behind her so I need to open it again to follow her. I have no idea how to live here any more.

We walk in the coffeehouse a few seconds apart and I spot Lucie going towards the back, away from Victor who is sitting at a table right by the door. I am so angry at Lucie for making me feel bad when I did nothing wrong, that I storm over to Victor's table myself. There he is, as usual, a pile of books from the University pushed aside so that he can lean his elbows on the table and read the newspaper.

"May I sit here?" I ask. I am looking at the back of his neck where his hair meets his skin. That spot, like the edge of Lac Léman, in Vevey, where it meets the shore, is everything at once.

He stands up and pulls out the chair for me. I sit down and look around to make sure Lucie knows I don't need her, but she is gone.

There is a glass wall that separates the tables, Jews on one side, everyone else on the other. It makes us feel we are integrated without having to test it out. Victor acts as if me sitting on this side of the wall is normal, which it most definitely is not. My hot chest and prickly eyes from fighting with Lucie spread out a little and I worry I will melt on the table top.

"What brings you here this evening?" Victor asks, as though we were picking up a conversation we had previously placed on the table, lifeless and waiting for us to revive it.

"Walking home from Dianabad." Which is not on the way from or to anywhere, and so lets him know exactly what I am doing here, without me saying it directly. Innuendo, suspense, tension – this is what I learned in Vevey.

"You are not at the Opera tonight?" It is all I can come up with.

"How did you know I love the Opera?"

"I have been watching you. I have seen you devour the reviews." Perhaps that is telling him too much, but it is too late.

"You like the music?" Victor says.

"Of course, but not as well as the stories."

"Do you listen to Strauss?" he asks.

"Of course."

"Do you like to dance?"

"Of course."

I am not being helpful, and I know it. I can see he is trying to find a place to rest the conversation, a way to extend it.

"I go to the Opera whenever I can," I say, doing as Lucie says and smiling hopefully at him, letting my eyes tell him that the Opera is not the only thing on my mind.

"Let's go together," he says.

We both deflate with relief. He said it, and

now we can talk. I ask him about his classes, and he gestures at the newspaper on the table and tells me that he loves them and wishes that history wasn't getting in the way. His father is not so happy with Victor's belief that we should fight Germany no matter what the cost.

"He just wants peaceful old age. He doesn't care who is in power as long as he can rake his rose garden and clip his precious blooms."

There is a war in me, a war just as sure as we sit here in Vienna and wait for Germany to invade. As sure as in the facts Victor is trying to pin down by scouring several papers a day. There is a war waging between the Alice sitting here now, who has been away and come back, and the place I have come back to and how I am supposed to behave here.

To say that I have had two lives, or to say that my life as Pup's nanny was an adventure, would be to pour so much cream in the coffee that you could barely taste the rough bitter edges of the flavor. There are not adjectives to describe how love moved through that house. It was in the lake, the shore, the house, the people, the words, the food – love was the vivifying force of everything at Villa Kenwin.

Vienna is a watermark, as on stationery. Above it is the head. Below, the stomach. The heart has no place in Vienna. There is no place here for Gryphon's hand slipped inside Kat's robe. No place for a *ménage* like Kenwin. No place for the raging feelings of desire that awoke in me there. If I unleash them here, I will set fire to the city.

My return to the Vienna of my childhood has turned me into a shadow of my Kenwin self. Kat and Gryphon hope psychoanalysis, or what they call ps-a, will free me from the conflict, but I am not so sure the whole problem is within me. They are great students of Dr. Freud. Gryphon pays for me to see Dr. Jekels. She thinks I learned her life, their lives, better than I did. She may believe I learned how to act on all that desire, but it is not true. I learned to live with it, to watch it, to crave it, to study it from afar, and to feel that life is pale without it, but I did not learn how to wield it to satisfy myself.

Dr. Jekels takes up residence in my head now, a part of the Kenwin life, the true life, where I can say what I want. Where people live by desire. Even he cannot solve my problem of feeling as if my very nature is corrupted now that I am back. This treatment feels to me the same as the way the girls at school would treat me and Lucie and the other Jewish girls – like our heritage was some superficial weakness we could get over if we tried hard enough. It never dawned on them that we might like being Jewish and that they were the ones with the problem. Maybe that, or perhaps I don't want to fix this swell in me that brings what is below the waterline right up into my heart and blocks any access at all to my head.

My sister Klara hopes Dr. Jekels will fix what has been broken in me. What has been cracked open. I hope that too. I just don't think that she thought it would involve me sitting in a café with this man, late for dinner, and staring at his jaw wondering if he has the nerve to do the things to me I have seen and am waiting to feel. But to me, doing those things? That would mean success.

Chapter 4

Klara and I go to have tea with Kat at her hotel. Kat wanted a copy of a certain Magnus Hirschfeld magazine. Klara brought it with trepidation from the bookstore where she works. It is filled with drawings of what Klara calls "degenerates." If she only knew where our mother sent me to work, she would faint. In the drawings there are men dressed as women married to women dressed as men. Old women in trousers and fake beards. Nothing really compares to scenes Kat has drawn for me in letters from Kenwin. Elisabeth Bergner, the actress Klara likes so much, sitting in the library at Kenwin in a suit and tie smoking a cigar with Gryphon in a men's dressing gown. She is so beautiful, Bergner, with her wide lips generously waiting for attention and her eyes so wide and clear. Her cheeks, begging for Gryphon to touch them along the prominent ridge of her cheekbone, sweep up in promise. None of this would make sense to Klara, who does not want women to hold cigars or promise. Of course, the way Klara holds the magazine, wrapped in brown paper as thought it might be contagious, lets me know this may be a difficult afternoon. She has never met Kat, and I wonder if this will set them against each other.

We arrive and Kat has a real English tea set out with jam, still in the cardboard box it was shipped in from London. Real, sticky sweet strawberry jam, and toast, and a pot of tea and cream. We put both butter and jam on the toast and eat each toast point in two bites. Very unladylike of Klara, but I decide not to mention it. She has forgiven Kat the magazine, so I am quiet. Klara is nervous, and Kat is watching her with interest. I can see Kat's eyes take in Klara's face, her worn dress, and her hair, primly up in a bun.

"You should cut your hair off," Kat says after a while.

"I am sorry Miss Doolittle, I can never do that," Klara says in her best English.

"*Could,* Klara, not *can,*" I tell her.

"Either way, you have the most remarkable

face, like a sweet gorgeous little boy, and it would look perfect with a short bob. Your eyes are so blue and your hair so dark, it would be striking."

"Thank you with the compliment."

"*For,* Klara, *for* the compliment," I am beginning to feel the back of my arms burn a little.

I am upsetting Klara, who will soon stop talking altogether, which is subconsciously my goal. She is used to being the smartest person in any room, with her access to all those books and her quick mind, but she would be no match for Kat even if I were not torturing her.

"What about me Kat, do you like my hair long?" I ask, hoping for a compliment. Kat loves my hair; she spent hours at Kenwin with a brush and oil, stroking it until it gleamed black and shiny. But she continues with Klara.

"So, do you know Dr. Freud?" Kat asks.

"No, but I have met his wife. She comes into the shop where I work one day last month."

"*Came.*"

"Came into the shop for a book. A cookery book. She has a guest, Heinrich Mann, the brother of the other writer, and he wants a German food."

"Dish, German *dish."*

Kat shoots me a look that says, settle down Alice.

"He wants a German dish, and she must make it, so she buys the book. A week later, she comes back. Heinrich Mann is happy with the food, the dish, and she must thank me. Such *Gemütlichkeit."*

"Coziness," I say and eat the last piece of toast.

Kat has brought us clothes from Kenwin. She knows that Klara's job at the bookstore and Ernst's at the bank support all of us while I study and mother does nothing. I let Klara take most of the clothes for herself, but I beg for a grey dress, just a bit less blue and more grey than Kat's eyes. It is simple, cut on the bias. Once Klara is done with alterations, it will look ravishing.

Flustered, Kat talks to us about exchanging money, and how she has gotten advice from one of Papa Freud's nephews about how to turn her Swiss money, which still has value, to Austrian currency, which has almost none. Klara begs her to let Ernst take care of it at the bank and save her the worry, and Kat gladly accepts, letting us know that if there is money to be made on the transaction, it is his. I don't think that was what Klara had in mind, and she is embarrassed to look like she is digging for gold.

Finally Kat pulls a dozen matchbooks out of her suitcase that Gryphon has saved for me. They are the colors of old Austria, all black and yellow. When I returned from Kenwin, I had several matchbooks, but even using just one match a week, I finished them all. They are a moment of color in an otherwise bleak landscape.

We leave with promises of tea every week while Kat is here in Vienna. She will come meet our mother as soon as she can. As we walk out the door, Kat pulls me back and swats me.

"Be nice," is all she says to me. "Alice, be *nice."*

Chapter 5

Once, at Villa Kenwin when I was taking care of Pup, I stayed up late with her because she could not sleep. She was filled with night terrors. There were monsters under her bed, in the closet, and under the sink in the bathroom. Lights had to be left on and the doors shut in a certain order so that the monsters could not get her and drag her to the underworld. Born in London in the shadow of the Great War, she had fear as a close companion.

Bedtime was difficult. Pup wanted to see and do everything and never miss a moment of life in the house. Often, the monsters helped her stay awake by putting so much fear in her that she bounced around her room, hitting several walls before she found the floor again.

"My mother made me hot milk with brandy when I could not sleep," I told her. "If you stay here under your covers, safe and quiet, I will make you some."

"What does it taste like, Alice?"

"A very grown-up drink, sweet and smooth. You will love it."

"Hand me Sweetie Bear and I will hold her till you get back."

I handed her the bear. Once white, it was now grey with a few darker spots, and I tucked the covers tight around her shoulders.

Having gotten me to hop, she relaxed.

I passed by Kat's room on my way to the kitchen and the light was on. I always looked in on Kat. Her erect back in her chair and the wild rapping of her typewriter thrilled me.

Kat could neither spell nor type clearly, then or now, but what comes out of her typewriter – poems, letters, stories – makes us all look at her sideways with greed and hunger when she is not watching. Everyone wants Kat's words to be about them.

Who is this woman we know so well from the words she writes? It seems unfair at times. I know so much about Kat and she knows nothing about me. I know intimate things, the way she sees colors. How she talks to the sea. The goddesses in the stories she reads to Pup. She doesn't ever tell me anything herself, but like Gryphon, I drink her words off the page, hoping I will be let inside. Kat always has a kind word for me, or a smile, and she is generous. But something in her holds back from everyone else, except when she writes. Then her vitality is focused on the page in front of her and her face becomes serene. The typewriter is where Kat is honest, where she puts all the ideas in her head that she only discusses with Gryphon. Gryphon knows each path of Kat's brain and can follow them to their end. Now, Dr. Jekels knows me that well. Analysis is like Kat's writing. Watching Kat type feels like spying until I read the words she puts on paper. When she pulls the page out with a flourish, willing to share it around, or when it appears in boxes of neatly lined-up blue cloth-bound books, and I can at last follow her words, I can feel the pulse in her fingers. Then I know she is kin to me.

That night, Gryphon sat beside Kat on the bed. As the owner of Kenwin, Gryphon was our patron – all of us, Kat, me, Dawg. She usually scared me a bit, when her fierce intellect and her command of German, English, French, Latin, Greek, and Arabic made me feel stupid. I wanted to communicate with anyone half as well in my own language as she did in all of those.

But, that night, Kat and Gryphon were silent.

The only light came from the lamp Kat loved, with the beaded fringe hanging from the deep red moiré, on the desk next to the typewriter. Kat's room was simple. Her clothes were neatly tucked away, her desk orderly: a pen next to the pile of paper on the blotter, her typewriter, and a book with a blue spine.

Gryphon wore an ancient blue Japanese kimono that she was given in Italy by her friend Norman Douglas. He wanted her to have something feminine she could actually wear. Gryphon loved to play at roles, the dapper Gryphon in a suit, the soft Gryphon in the robe; the stern mistress of Kenwin, the loving friend. That robe was to me a beacon from a far shore. A land inhabited by people who knew the edges of their own skin.

Kat had her hair down, and it fell over her eyes as she rested on one elbow. Gryphon was looking down at Kat through her hair.

I stood still in the doorway to see closer. Gryphon traced Kat's lips with her finger and Kat shut her eyes to feel the touch. Gryphon ran her finger delicately over Kat's closed eyelid, who let her head fall back. She pushed Kat's hair aside and whispered something in Kat's ear. Kat opened her eyes and smiled. Gryphon slid her hand inside Kat's robe, between Kat's legs, resting it there softly. Gryphon's other hand was tracing Kat's lips now, her hand cupped around Kat's chin. Kat, who could be in motion while sitting in a chair reading a book, was still, languid, flushed. I could see the silk of Kat's robe move over Gryphon's hand. Kat's body tensed and her feet pointed. Kat licked Gryphon's finger, pulling it into her mouth, between her white teeth. While Gryphon's eyes went out of focus, Kat's became clear and penetrating. I was afraid she would see me, there through the sliver of door, so I backed up as Kat's breath sped up.

Gryphon moved her finger from Kat's lips and across her cheekbone. She said only one phrase low to Kat, a whisper, *"J'ai envie."* I desire you. I need you. I want you beyond what

I can say. Kat pulled Gryphon to her by tangling up her long fingers in Gryphon's hair. They kissed and slowly, Kat opened her mouth to let Gryphon in deeper.

I hurried to the kitchen, saying over and over to myself, *"J'ai envie."* I was not at all sorry I had seen them. I understood then that I am a Gryphon. What I want is to be the one who desires. *"J'ai envie."*

Women are not supposed to be that one. We are supposed to endure, passive, as things are done to us. I had always thought I'd live in that submissive state, but now I had this image of Kat lying on the bed, eager for desire to come – a fully-alive woman. Watching, it was as if I had crossed a threshold. I now knew that Kat, Gryphon and I are such women. I could touch someone someday the way Gryphon touched Kat.

As I heated the milk and warmed my hands from the heat of the stove, I felt as though a flame was ignited inside me. It rolled over my shoulders and down through my belly and between my legs. It has not gone out since.

Chapter 6

simply don't refuse when my mother insists Ernst come with me to the Altshul's for dinner. I am afraid to see Lucie, and he is good padding if her anger is still smoldering under the surface. When we arrive, Josef Altshul is sitting at the head of the table looking like a polished doll with his round belly, rosy cheeks, and all the buttons gleaming on his coat. His eyes are exactly like Lucie's, cinnamon-colored and glossy as they move around the table. They fix on each one of us for a moment, sliding from face to face, and in between dip to the lace tablecloth with concentric circles of roses worked into it, to the silver edging on the Delft plates that stand like an honor guard, to the cut crystal water and wine glasses in perfect marching order, and to the bowl of lilies in the center of the table. Unfortunately, the lilies are not tall enough to obscure my view of Lucie, making headlamps of her eyes as she talks to Ernst.

"Did you read the paper today, Ernst?" Papa Altshul asks. We all know what he is talking about. The NDSAP, the Nazis. Without waiting for a reply, he goes on, "We Jews cannot delude ourselves. That man's beating has to do with the NDSAP even if the paper says otherwise."

"The Chancellor is going to handle that," Ernst looks hopefully around at us.

Mr. Altshul waves the maid away as she comes to serve him fish. "No, no, he's not. He can't stop them from hating the idea of Jews while dismissing the real facts of our lives as irrelevant."

The maid places the plates in front of us and I can smell the savory whitefish, but the conversation has banished my appetite.

Ernst hopes if the Chancellor is tough on the NDSAP they will be disbanded, but he is wise enough to keep his mouth shut. No one is eating the fish, the white sauce that drapes it clumping up and cold. We are all waiting for something to happen, and while we cannot stop thinking about the beatings reported in the paper, each of us has a personal explanation for what is happening that makes it easier to understand. My own mother believes, as do many of her friends who hear news second-hand, that we are simply lucky not to be part of the class that labors and lives in reduced circumstances. That is where the violence happens. She thinks we are lucky not to be workers, and are safe from the hooligans who do this kind of violence.

"I find it important to look carefully at the facts and not let myself be led astray by opinion," Papa Altshul tells Ernst by way of telling all of us. "When I was a boy, there was a puppet show in the park, with a purportedly humorous moment in which the character dressed like a Chasid was beaten to death by the clown with a tiny stick. The clown kept hitting him, even after he fell over and waved his arms to stop. All the children were laughing as the Jew in the puppet theater shook with mock fear as the clown hit his head again and again. He shook one final time and lay still. All the children clapped."

The maid comes in with the next course and we are silent as she serves us our portions of chicken and perfect tiny button mushrooms, and takes away the fish, untouched.

"I get the feeling," Ernst says, "that everyone I know who is not Jewish, even my friends and colleagues, is secretly happy to see the anti-Semites gain footing. As though things would go better if they could just get us out of the way, but they are not yet willing to do it themselves."

Kat often wonders how it is I can be so thin here, where the food is so delicious and the pastry omnipresent. As I sit with my fork in hand, hovering above the plate, I cannot take a single bite. I would have to swallow around the fear lodged in my throat, my immediate fear that Ernst and Papa Altshul are right, and a deeper fear that Victor might feel as Ernst describes.

Mrs. Altshul has not said a word all evening. She sits with her perfectly coiffed silver hair tucked behind her ears, and her pearl earrings large enough to reflect a miniature version of the table back at you, feeling that the conversation has been led the wrong way. She wishes, down to the toes of her shiny black shoes, that we would speak about anything else. I know she believes as my mother does, that we will be spared all this by wealth or position, that we bring the real culture and art to this city, and that somehow we are more German than the Viennese around us. In our superiority we carry the torch of German culture in this city of pompous bureaucrats. She would never dare say this in front of her husband, so she pushes a small piece of chicken around her plate and does not make eye contact.

Lucie began dinner blatantly not talking to me. She was doing what I call tongue-on-tooth to show her anger. She puts her tongue against one of her back molars and sets her jaw and you feel the waves of resentment radiating from her. She is now looking down at the white linen napkin on her lap, edged with lace roses to match the tablecloth, smoothing it over and over against the tops of her thighs.

With his wise concern for ethics and his mind always turned to the facts, cutting through delusion, Papa Altshul reminds me of one of the Greek Stoic philosophers. He is capable of no foolishness, and is always trying to improve everyone around him, mind and body. He isn't vain, he despises conventionality, and his deepest concern is for what is true. When he speaks he is never superficial, always studied and serious. He raised Lucie to have perfect posture, to value a healthy body and mind, and above all to never seek anyone's favor or bow to them. If he believes that the NDSAP is behind all the beatings and the broken windows of Jewish stores, then I believe it also. If he believes the Chancellor can't stop the Parliament from self-destruction, or the violence from harming us, I believe that, too. If he believes this is not the petty tolerable hatred of a childhood puppet show, then I believe we have cause to worry.

Ernst has pushed his chair back and is holding his water glass by the stem like a child holds the string of a balloon to keep it from floating away. I am afraid he will snap it in two, as he hangs on to it to save his life.

The maid brings out a silver coffee set, steaming with the bitter roasted smell of coffee. In the other hand she balances a plate of her famous nut horns. The pastry is crumbly and buttery. The nuts are so finely ground they look like powdered sugar on top. I take one off the plate as she passes, and accept a demitasse of coffee. My stomach is Viennese, and tells me I will eat the cookie. My heart is beating out of time and it tells me I am more lonely here than I was speaking French in Vevey, many many miles from home.

I rest the cookie on the edge of my coffee cup and reach for the cream and sugar. Across the table Lucie is looking at me, and I smile at her weakly and apologetically. We touch fingers over the sugar bowl, and she nods. Suddenly we are fine. The vanilla filling of the nut horn oozes into my mouth and I allow myself the pleasure of licking every bit of it out with the tip of my tongue. I poke into the hole where the cream was and search for any bits I may have left behind. The cream, with floating specks of vanilla bean, is the warm soft yellowish color of perfect custard. I want to bathe in it. I dip the shell into my coffee and eat it quickly, before it melts away. The coffee makes my throat relax. The cream soothes the sharp feeling that I cannot swallow.

At the front door, Lucie hands me my coat, and her eyes look into mine. I see her as a four-year-old on the first day of kindergarten, holding a stuffed plush dog by the neck, not willing to part with it. She brought that dog to school for a long time. Eventually the dog moved to her pocket, then into her school bag, and one day she left it home. I wonder where it is now.

Excerpt from a Letter from H.D. to Kenneth
MacPherson, Hotel Regina, Vienna

March 4, 1933

"Alice asks of you. She is oddly and some-
what pathetically subdued here, poor darling,
I suppose HERE, she is jew-conscious, poor,
poor, girl. I took her to a quaint little wine
shop restaurant, where she ate more than I
ever saw her eat, even the ham, rather rak-
ishly. She told me she had seldom been to a
"real" restaurant in Vienna, more often in
communal studenten barracks pubs. I don't
know if she is verboten, or if it is a question
of dollars, anyhow, I am touched and rather
upset by this new, much thinner, subdued
Alice, so unlike the old swash-buckling
[one]…"

Chapter 7

We are all surprised Kat came to see Papa Freud after Hitler was made Chancellor in Germany. We are so frightened of what is happening: the fighting, the army in the street looking at every clump of four people as a potential mob. What did that book say? Don't be too interesting or intelligent in Vienna, they might think you're a Jew. I can't stand the thought of Kat stopped by soldiers, or anyone else. I try to come to her hotel in time to walk her to ps-a every day, as though my presence will make her safer as she walks to Papa Freud's office. What they talk about I have no idea, but the rumor is she is his most favorite patient. Anyhow, it is electric to turn the corner of Papa Freud's street and leave Kat to him. The meeting of the geniuses.

Pup, Kat reminds me, is thirteen this month. She is on a cruise with Mouse, our neighbor at Kenwin, another British lady who has escaped England to live by herself and read books. There seem to be an endless supply of these. Pup is happy, Kat says, happy to be sailing around Greece looking at pretty, old things. Kat is happy to have her see them before it is too late. That is how she is talking, and how Gryphon's letters read. Before it is too late.

Kat took me to a restaurant I'd never seen before. On the walls hung paintings of village scenes, old chalets halfway up a hill or next to a babbling brook. An oil painting of a large red apple in a basket next to a brown jug graced another wall, aged by smoke and cooking oil. There were also blue plates mounted above the doors and painted with scenes of sawmills and rushing rivers. The waiters were dressed like 18th century peasants. The cuisine was all meant to be Austrian country food. I ate so much I embarrassed myself. With Kat I manage to get food past the knot in my throat.

"Look at that one," Kat points at a painting of a bridge across a river with a bright cheerful forest on the other side. "It doesn't feel like that when you see it. I was in Innsbruck in

1913 with my mother."

"Where was your father?"

"He said he had to go back to America to get shoes."

"Shoes?"

"It could have been something else, I was young, but that's what I remember. We went to a village just like that one and they were doing the Passion Play. I was frightened by the costumes and the masks that made everyone look like a puppet. There were wooden carvings of Christ writhing on the cross everywhere I looked and they had the most tortured faces; I couldn't stand seeing him that way. He looked like he knew just how bad the world was and that what he was doing would make no difference, and that the fact hurt him more than the nails and thorns. I broke away from my mother and dashed across the bridge to hide in the forest. In Pennsylvania, we have warm, kind forests with tall deciduous trees and you can see the sky. This forest was ominous. I could barely get into it, and when I did, I was lost right away."

"What happened? Who found you?"

"My mother was talking to a woman by the

bridge – she spoke perfect German –" here Kat bows her head to acknowledge that she does not, "and the woman just reached into the forest and pulled me out. It seemed to me she never even stepped in herself, her arm just knew where to go. She insisted that we go back to her house and have tea. She had some sort of inn she ran out of her house, and she thought we were British, so she made the worst weak tea I have ever tasted. But, she had a painting of the Emperor in his military regalia and the Empress sat beside him in a midnight blue décolleté gown and pearls. She looked just like the Empress on Tarot cards. She was gorgeous, regal, earthy, and very high-minded. I wanted to grow up to be her."

I did not know what to say. If our places were switched, Kat, with her American enthusiasm, would have thrown her arms around me and told me I was the Empress. But all I could do was smile.

"Look, Alice, I understand what is going on here." She does not say any of the dangerous words.

All I can do is nod, the food heavy now in my stomach.

"I promise that Gryphon is doing everything she can to get people in England worried about Hitler." As she tells me this, she looks over my head at the ceiling and her shoulders hunch. She doesn't have to say it. I know Gryphon is having no success.

"She is trying." Kat says.

"I'm glad. She will make someone listen. Gryphon will take charge."

"We hope, but there are so many rumors here, so much going on that they refuse to see."

"Because of us?"

"Because no one wants to think there will be another war. Unimaginable."

It is impossible, sitting in the restaurant, to envision war. All the glasses are reflecting light like so many diamonds scattered around the room. The silverware makes twinkling noises as it touches the plates. The waiters are in little coats and pants that button on the sides. There are silver covers on the dishes. I have not seen anything like this since before I went to Kenwin, before the banks collapsed, before my father died.

Chapter 8

I bring Kat to the coffeehouse where Victor goes. There, she can read all the papers and sit for hours watching people. Kat is so grateful because she feels cut off from the news when Gryphon is not around. I am surprised how well she reads German, I don't remember knowing that about her. I am glad that she speaks so poorly so that I can be in charge of her, at least in a small way. We drink our cups of sweet coffee and we watch the people as they filter in, sit, read, talk, and filter out. Kat does not like it here in Vienna. I know Gryphon hates it, she much prefers the temperament of people in Berlin. She told me the first time she met me that she felt it was too Southern here, whatever she meant by that. Kat is more open to the world and, because I've read every word she's published, and every book she sends me, I see Vienna through her eyes – so fat and cold. Papa Freud and his Berggasse 19 are the only bright spots.

Kat never saw me as a Jew in Switzerland, but here she is worried about me. She sits at the table and watches how the waiters look at me. She feels that glass wall separating me from the other patrons. Kat can tell that this mixing up of people and cultures is a sham. We are as separate as if we lived in a ghetto. I watch to see if any waiter hesitates before he tips his head and says "Fraulein?" No one does. Not today. It would have been so much worse to be ignored, passed over for the next customer, while Kat watched. I could not have stood it. Normally, I simply read the paper and wait. Gryphon taught me never to give in just because someone thinks less of who I am.

Years ago, when Gryphon simply stopped wearing dresses altogether, I thought for sure that when she went into Vevey for the post or even to London to see her parents at Bryaudley, she would return cowed. But she never showed a sign of concern for anything other than finding the best material for her suits, the best tailor, the right buttons. It was pure delight to see her get fitted. She fingered the fabrics, watched them drape over her, touched the thread. Gryphon never acknowledged that what she was asking for, to be dressed in pants and a jacket, was an odd request for a woman.

No one has ever said a word to her about her clothes in front of me, nor have I have heard of anyone saying anything behind her back. She does everything with a sense of sureness and walks into any room as if she cannot wait to see what it will present to her. I usually feel turned inside out when I have to speak to anyone I don't know, but Gryphon is the opposite. She has always seen each new person and each new situation as a package waiting to be unwrapped, not a catastrophe waiting to happen.

Because of Gryphon, I sit in the coffeehouse until someone comes and takes an order. I smile and wave to my friends, read a newspaper, leave if I have an appointment. I come back the next time. If I never get coffee, then that is simply the way it is. Kat does not know that. She does not know that I have to use what I learned at Kenwin. But from her letters I know Kat and Gryphon see me as a Jew in a dangerous time. What does dangerous mean? They are worried about Europe, about War, about Politics. They see maps and borders and events. Gryphon is trying to get people in England worried about

Germany, worried about the chance that the end of the Great War will not be an end to fighting, but no one will listen.

"I believe you need to leave here," Kat says very quietly.

"Come to Kenwin?"

"Anywhere is safer than here. You and Papa Freud. Your family and his."

"You make my heart beat faster, Kat."

"I want to see you all safe from the spreading darkness."

Victor walks in while we are talking and goes to the bar to order a coffee and find a paper. It is uncanny, because my next thought, after soaring into Kenwin with Kat, is of Victor. Of my heart smashed to bits leaving him here. In my mind we are so close, he and I. It is like one of Papa Freud's dreams where the actions are all in a jumble but infinitely interconnected. Pull on one end and you displace things all along the line. I watch the back of his head. His blonde hair looks so full from the back. The pale skin below it smells like soap, I am sure. He is wearing a green woolen jacket that smells like tobacco smoke. I can smell his stained fingers, though his back is to me across the room.

"You look much brighter." Kat said to me. "Our swashbuckling Alice."

"I feel glad that you want me back at Kenwin," I told her, watching Victor over her shoulder.

I am not the Alice from Villa Kenwin. The Alice from Kenwin would have brought him to the table. I fell in love easily there, with every passing writer and visitor, with the boy who delivered the mail, with the stationmaster and his beautiful moustache. But none of it ever went anywhere. That doesn't mean I didn't drive Kat crazy talking to her about all of them, but this is different. He is not Jewish. He is older than I. What does not matter to Kat and to the world of Kenwin would kill my mother. My family, everyone we know, the whole city of Vienna sits astride me and compresses my ribs so that I can barely take in air.

Instead, I go to get Kat a new paper and I brush against his arm as I walk by. I make sure that my hip grazes his sleeve and I give my best welcoming smile. Lucie would be proud. Lucie would like the Kenwin Alice better than she likes her dear old friend.

"Come back tomorrow, I have tickets," is all he says to me.

Chapter 9

I tell Dr. J of a dream I have. Victor is standing above me at the foot of my bed. He is naked. I am not able to see him clearly because the room is in shadows. I am lying on the bed I had at Villa Kenwin, not the one I share here with Klara. His presence, his smell, the feeling of his eyes as they touch my body tell me something fierce is living in him. I cannot see his face, but I see that I am having an effect on him. His body is responding to me, as mine is to him. My hand moves of its own accord and throws off the sheets and lifts up my nightgown. Victor watches me as if he might at any second take a bite of me. I start by taking off my drawers. Then I show him my breasts and stomach. My hands run flat over them, doing for him what he cannot do himself. Making my nipples stand out, showing the hollow as my stomach slopes into my hips, parting myself for him to see.

It is as though he is on the other side of a

wall and can see me, but cannot reach out to me. Something magical must happen for him to get to me. I must make this magic.

I feel my hip bones jut out in front of me as I move myself up and down, pressing into the featherbed and up again. A rhythm emerges, slow and mesmerizing to Victor. My fingers, my hand, my legs spreading, inviting him, my pupils dilating, my breathing becoming shallow. I can see him in my mind ripping my flesh off with his teeth and consuming me.

I run my hand between my legs and my hand becomes his hand, the fingers emerge wet. He fills me with his fingers, delicate and tobacco stained. I know they taste bitter and salty from sweat and smoke. If I put his thumb in my mouth and suck gently I could clean off all residue and taste only him. His thumb is on the outside taking over the rhythm my hips made, making it his own. Slipping his longest finger inside of me and cupping me with his hand, he fills that space in me I know is endless and could swallow us. We rock together and as I feel heat spreading in my palms and the soles of my feet, he starts to disappear again. He becomes vapor, fingers, mist, movement, music floating in from the street below. I explode into a thousand stars.

We are floating above the riverbed, coursing with floodwater, overflowing the concrete banks. We block the constellations from the sky, leaving patches of darkness shaped like entwined lovers, shaped like his muscled body and mine. Then I wake up in my bed and it is raining. The first rain of spring.

Dr. Jekels responds to the dream by saying "You identify too much with women like Kat and Gryphon."

"I do not," I say, sounding like Pup gearing up for a tantrum. "I really don't. Maybe with Gryphon, but not with Kat."

"She is a displaced father figure, Gryphon. Your job is to wrest your identification from the father and place it squarely on the mother." He points out that my father is dead, which comes up every time my back rests on the couch.

"That is not what Herr Doktor Freud is telling Kat."

"Maybe not, but that is what I am telling you."

I see Herr Doktor Jekels for a moment as an

elderly, dapper, Jewish man with well-trimmed silver hair and a gold watch chain slinking across his vest. He is no longer the trickster jaguar god of the underworld, he is a product of the same world that made my mother into a woman who has yet to tell me that love exists, or to warn me about physical attraction. She is the woman who turned Klara into an old maid while we both still live at home sharing the same bed we did as children.

Dr. J understands Kat is a patient of Papa Freud's and Gryphon of Dr. Sachs'. He would not presume, but Papa himself, before he met Kat, said women like that simply have not resolved their Oedipal complexes. He is telling Kat different things now, but maybe Dr. J does not know that.

"Women who write," he keeps explaining, "need somehow to be men. They want to exert too much influence on the world. They want to take a place in the world that is not open to them and they create friction for themselves, unnecessary heartache. You don't need to do that, Alice. Women like Kat and Gryphon are too much in the world. When they do resolve to be like their mothers, they will find men and be normal."

"I am in love with Victor, who is, after all, a man."

"Your love of Victor is unnatural. Heated. You are running away from being a woman."

"From what?" I ask, genuinely interested in how I could possibly run away from being a woman any easier than I could from, say, being a Jew.

"From your life. From finding a husband, having children, growing up. Alice, this is not only impossible, it is dangerous for you and for him. There has never been an easy place for us to live, and this moment is a difficult one. Don't bring the weight of history down on your head to satisfy your neurosis. It is not Victor you want anyhow, and we both know that."

"But I'm happy." I say weakly.

"No, you are obsessed. Let him go and settle down with someone who can bring you happiness inside the life you know."

"Then you really don't understand," I say.

He tells me less Kat and more Klara would make me a happier neurotic.

Chapter 10

I meet Victor at the coffeehouse. He talks to me so kindly I feel a glimmer of Kenwin in his voice. He pulls out my chair for me and I feel like looking around to see if anyone saw. But, the coffehouse was the same as any other day, and a group of men arguing politics at the table next to us are so loud and insistent that Victor has to move his chair closer so we can hear each other. I feel as worried as they do about the fascists, about Hitler, about the tightening measures the government is taking, but I can only focus on Victor, looking so smooth and freshly shaven. I smell the soap on his chin and see where his face is pink from the razor. He blushes.

"So. I went to a boy's school, I haven't talked to women much."

"What about swimming?"

"That is different, they are athletes, but my team is all men."

"Don't you have any sisters?"

"No, and if I did, that would be different."

"Please, don't think of me as a sister," I smile at him and realize I am scaring him.

"No, this is, well, this is what I prayed for when I was younger."

"What? Going to the Opera with a Jew?"

"I prayed that I would get to touch a girl before I died. It seemed so impossible that it would ever happen."

He brushes his hand against mine on the table. There is a spark when we touch. I had not figured him to be this innocent, and it annoys me. I push my foot against his under the table and smile at him. I want him to know it is okay, and I am afraid if I say anything out loud, I will insult him.

He loves the Opera. We go on student tickets and sit very far back and see Die Götterdämmerung. That, Klara understands. Even my mother understands. I had no trouble leaving the house tonight. I just left Victor out of the story. The Opera is for good girls. I don't feel safe, even with Victor, because the walk there is filled with fear of getting stuck in the wrong place at the wrong time. I can't tell who the good guys are, as everyone is out of their heads with anger and fear. Victor hurries me down the street and through the light spilling out of open doors into the lobby.

Inside, the Opera is crowded and the air is hot. People are milling about and the orchestra is warming up, running scales up and down. I feel shivers in my back when I hear the bassoon. The sound is so low it vibrates my body. The seats are smaller toward the back and once we settle in the lights dim. In the dark I feel faint, feel the heat of his shoulder as I lean into it. I am drifting off into a dream of Victor standing in his swimsuit by the edge of the river, about to dive in, and on the other side, blurry but discernable, the trees are waving. His chest is dripping with water and he smiles at me before he dives. I push harder against his shoulder. He apologizes and moves a bit to allow me more space. I want the opposite. I move my leg so our knees touch and he crosses his legs to make room for me. The Norns are singing about fate, about how the past, present, and future weave together. About how Wotan will set fire to Valhalla and signal the end of the gods and as the rope breaks on stage, I think maybe this is exactly where we are. If Hitler was smart, he wouldn't blame the Reichstag fire on the communists, he would use this myth to proclaim himself the inheritor of the earth now that the time of the gods has ended. The rope that was woven out of our shared experience here in Vienna has snapped, as if Hitler himself cut it, and now we move forward in a godless age.

As the Rhine flows on stage, I feel my legs grow warm. I want to be submerged in the music and let my hair flow behind me. Victor is swimming in the river below, and the maidens are stroking him from shoulder to hip as he moves by. The Rhinemaidens reclaim the ring, cleansed of its curse. They are submerged in the water with long blonde hair behind them. In my mind they are doing things to Victor that make him blush. They loosen his tie, they swim next to him and brush their bodies along his, and all the while he looks at them as if to say, "Me? Really?"

The cool water cleanses them of lust and sin. They are some ideal of womanhood. No one would write an opera about lustful Jewish girls who squirm in their beds at night wanting to be touched.

At the interval, we stand and stretch. Victor talks mostly about politics, as does everyone else I know. He invites me to come to a meeting to discuss what is happening.

"These are smart people," he tells me.

"Smart enough to make it stop?"

"Not sure anyone can do that now Alice, but smart enough to understand what is happening."

"Any fool can see that Dolfuss is frightened. Hitler is angry that his home country is ignoring his party. The country is out of money, and we are all living like pieces on a chess board, or something more sinister."

He smiles at me and takes my fingers in his hand. He touches them to his lips. Neither of us mention the obvious.

I ask if I can bring Kat. I know she would want to go. Gryphon writes us both horrific letters about Hitler and what he is doing, and how the English will not respond. She is furious and has printed up copies of *J'Accuse* to pass out to everyone she can. Victor says, "Well, she is right." I know she is, and I am petrified.

"Nothing good can possibly come of this,"

Victor says ominously. The lights flash for us to sit down.

"I am so frightened by this I can't think straight to talk about it," I say.

"Come to the meeting. It may help to see that other people are as worried as you."

When we sit back down, I simply take Victor's hand and put it on my leg. He looks around to see if anyone is looking at us, but the lights go down and he relaxes.

"You can touch me, it's okay," I whisper as quietly as possible.

"So. You are a dream come true," he says.

I have seen Dawg tell his black boys, "Upstairs," and wink at Kat and Gryphon and leave. I have pictures in my mind of what they do. I know what lust looks like when I see it, and Victor has that out of focus look to his eyes that tells me I am not alone in wishing the ring would go ahead and be dealt with so we can be alone.

But, we are never alone. Even in the dark. Even in my unconscious, Dr. J is there. I hear him in my head telling me this is not a good idea. That I am not in love. That I am using Victor to externalize a conflict I need to work out in ps-a. I am afraid I will stand up in the middle of the singing and scream, "This is my life! I get to live it however I want. No analyst, no politicians, no sisters, no mother can tell me what to do!"

The fantasy is so real I am shocked when the music is still playing and everyone is facing forward. I lean my head against Victor's shoulder and he touches my hair softly. It may not be a loud romp in the upstairs bedroom at Kenwin, but I feel his desire for me in the dark with the music flowing around us. It is as soft and tangible as satin.

Letter from H.D. to Bryher
Hotel Regina, Vienna
March 11, 1933

"A. told me a long tale of how Dr. J. was trying to interfere in her private life and I said 'Good, Freud says you can't be helped unless you have a real resistance.'"

Excerpt from a letter from H.D. to Bryher
Hotel Regina, Vienna
March 19, 1933

"Here, Alice is so different, she speaks hardly to anyone, looks frightened in restaurants, I imagine her whole Kenwin and Hellenics phase of arrogance was sheer reaction from the home-town. She is speechless and proper and respectful, unless it is ps-a at work. She is cross with Jekels as she started to tell me she had fallen in love and it worried her, then she realized that I heard that 20 times, and J. told her she was not REALLY in love with this person but trying to escape something. Of course, we all know that. But A. was half in mood for spilling her love-affair... This was about 4:30. She walked me down to 19 Berg, wanted to talk and didn't, about her 'affair.' But I don't want to butt in, don't want to remind her she told me of at least a half dozen of these terrible love crises..."

Much, much, much, much, love and thanks always,

Kat.

Chapter 11

Kat and I are getting ready to go to the meeting. Her back is to me and she is brushing her hair at the mirrored dresser and putting a scarf around her neck. I am aware that for so many people she is a symbol of the feminine principle, a goddess bringing back the idea of divinity to the world. I am also wondering if she will get sick of the jacket she is wearing, made of fabric that glimmers in the lamplight, and give it to me. I have so many of her clothes; they are cast-offs to her, but when I wear them I feel I have a chance that someday someone will gaze at me like Gryphon gazes at her. I have to have Klara cut them down as I am not as tall or as broad as Kat, but I feel bigger in her clothes.

Dr. Jekels knows about Victor and he is not happy. I tell Kat and she shrugs and looks over her shoulder at me and pouts her lips as if to say, that is his job.

"He thinks that I am fixated. He thinks that I need to find a man my age, which is a diversion, as Victor is maybe five years older than me. A boy then, he means, a Jewish boy, and get married. He has told me to stop thinking about Victor even if I must change where I go, who I see."

"You are fixated, Alice."

"Is there anything wrong with that?"

"No, unless you are unwilling to look at it."

"I am looking and I like what I see."

"You know exactly what I mean. Look at yourself and see where it all comes from. Understand on a level where you are not fooling yourself. Know thyself, γνώριζε τον εαυτό σου."

"You sound like Dr. J. Greek and all. You flirt and fling and no one asks you to do anything differently."

"I don't need to be asked. I want to get free of the things I don't understand and use them to make more energy in my life. I go into Papa's office and try to connect it all for him — the dreams, the memories of my Grandfather making clay sheep for us at Christmas time, the fact that Papa Freud reminds me of D.H.

Lawrence. I treat him like a prophet, and I want to be his priestess and drink from the vial that will let me shift shapes. What I see in you is that you are trapped in spinning circles. Where is this going to go with Victor? What can you possibly do about it? You want what you cannot possibly have, and you refuse to face that aspect of your life. There is a difference between living from your desires and using desire to avoid your life."

I cannot believe she is telling me this. She sounds exactly like Dr. J, and I hate him for telling me this. I think Dr. J is just like my family. "Find a Jewish boy and have a family of your own."

Even now, when the world is in such turmoil. When we are all so lost to reason. Of course it is not going anywhere, nothing is going anywhere but to hell. I might as well die having made love to Victor as not. But Dr. J thinks this is just another fascinating dream I have, a way of twisting the present to meet my fantasy of being Kat. I choose not to tell her that part.

I can see Dr. J sitting in the parlor with my mother having coffee and pastries, nodding.

Being so calm when that particular kind of calm is dying out in the world. They will talk about what to do with me, and agree to auction me off to the highest bidder. I can make grandchildren and name them after my grandparents and push a pram around, looking smug. I can ask my mother for advice about diapers and colic since she is useless when it comes to love and war.

Kat says, "Hating Dr. Jekels is reasonable. As reasonable as the unconscious can be. I was worried you felt nothing for Dr. Jekels at all. That could have been a sign of real neurosis. Hating him might get you cured faster. Loving him is the slow, painful but thorough, way to a cure."

She is clearly talking about loving Papa Freud. I want to tell her loving Victor is making my heart move in my chest. In a way that feels frightening. In a way I have to do something about. I want to tell her this time it is different than all the other times I have felt something. This time I cannot escape the tidal pull towards him. There is a force outside my body that controls me.

Kat and I go to an apartment in a socialist

building. We have been told what time to arrive. Everyone is to come in dribs and drabs so that it does not look like too many people are congregating at once. The building is concrete, new architecture, and we stop for a moment to admire how functional it is, how devoid of unnecessary decoration. It reminds me of Kenwin. Someone once described it as architecture without eyebrows.

Inside, the living room is packed with people. I see Victor standing in the doorway to the kitchen. He waves and tries to make his way over to us, but people stop him to talk. Kat wants to talk about the parliament, and what Dolfuss is doing, and how disbanding them couldn't possibly help.

"I know it's American of me," she says, "But I don't understand how suspending democracy could help restore it."

I translate for her so that she can talk to Victor when he joins us.

"I don't think he is worried about democracy, I think he is worried about fights in the streets and broken bottles everywhere and people afraid to go out of their houses."

"Why isn't anyone out demanding that the

NDSAP retreat?"

"They are. But it's not just them, everyone is fighting everyone, and the violence is just getting worse." I realize we are whispering half in English and half in German and everyone is looking at us. Kat notices too but her German's not good enough for what she is trying to say.

"After Hitler was elected, we wanted to bring you back to Kenwin."

"Bring me back, please," I say in English so that only Kat can understand.

The meeting starts and people are asking questions. I quietly translate into English what I think Kat will miss in German. Phrases about martial law and how the Reichstag fire was not set by communists. I am at a loss for the English word for prison camp, but Kat nods and whispers to me,

"Gryphon knew about that. Communists and Jews are to be sent there but no one believed her."

"There is no rational reason for it," I say.

The voices swell around us, not saying anything I can take in. These are mostly Christian intellectual Marxists who are scared about how Dolfuss is making a Christian capitalist machine out of their beloved homeland. One man stands up and says,

"There is nothing we can do about it but endure."

The room is silent.

"Hitler is a phase. The country will survive this, or we will get swallowed by Germany. Either way, we endure."

The room erupts in a roar of people arguing. I stare at the faces, so wild and agitated, and these are the reasonable people. One man is in rolled-up shirtsleeves and a vest, his forearms bare and his hands clenching and unclenching. As he talks, his face gets redder and redder. I wonder what Papa Altshul would say if he were here — his low loud voice calming everyone down and making us assess the situation piece by piece. But even when you do that, all the pieces don't add up. The next man to speak wants to discuss how Dolfuss is signing secret treaties with France and there is no point to it as it only angers Germany and does us no good. The man after him wants to talk about how Hitler is organizing the youth, and it looks an awful lot like indoctrination.

The next man talks about the world economy and how we are too small to survive the depression, especially with Hitler taxing German citizens who come into Austria. He is answered by someone who says tourism in the country is not going to do anything but make us more quaint and rural and resistant to a workers revolution. I get lost trying to find the right words for Kat. The English I know all has to do with poetry. Poetry and love.

Excerpt from a letter from H.D. to Bryher
Hotel Regina, Vienna
March 22, 1933

"I had already had an hour and a half of political meeting here with Alice. She confided to me that she and her sister were simply shaking all over, all the time. She said they pretended it couldn't matter but they were terrified. I put it down to the anti-s. [anti-semitism] and said so, but A. denied it, said it was the world crisis, seeing men suddenly lost to reason, etc."

Chapter 12

I wake in the night sweating, having taken off my nightdress in my sleep. I am naked beside Klara, lying on soaked sheets. This is not a fit of erotic pleasure; my heart is beating irregularly and I am crying. The smallest difficulty, a lost pen or a dropped book, now makes me break into tears of frustration and fury. Dr. Jekels applauds this. "Oh, oh," he says, "it is breaking through."

I cannot do the simplest things – mix up a cake, make coffee. I burn everything and let the coffee go until it is bitter and serve it anyway. The only thing that makes me feel any better is being with Victor. I pretend to be the perfect woman, and then I am. I am once again beguiling and attractive and not at all frightened and unable to breathe correctly.

It is hard to be in Vienna now. Even Kat notices it. She talks of the soldiers in the streets and the concern Gryphon has for Papa Freud. Gryphon is starting to plot getting us all out of here. Kat thinks that is the only problem. She does not feel the weight of the paving stones on her back as she sleeps.

I turn over in bed at night and Klara is sleeping waveless beside me. In and out, in and out, her breath smooth. I know she is scared too, I can feel it from her when she is awake. We move around the apartment trying to avoid each other. Ernst is studying wildly to finish his degree, he worries that they will forbid Jews to go to the University before he finishes, or that he will lose his job at the bank and we will starve. Dolfuss's new constitution seems to allow freedom of religion, but I think this is to strengthen theirs, not preserve ours.

I never fit here. In this city, in this family, in this flat. Not even at the University where the most radical are still too serious. No humor. No light. Kenwin is full of light and jest and nick-names. Jokes. Even at people's expense. Even the Quex, the Dragon housekeeper of Kenwin, who we all fear, makes us laugh at our own infirmities. She steals the good wine and scrimps on the sugar and scares away book editors from America.

One day, when I returned early from Vevey,

having left Pup with the Mouse next door, I came upon the Quex in the kitchen. She had our beloved Norman Douglas pressed against the sink with her fury. He had a bottle of something in his hand, and the liquor cupboard was gaping. She was screaming at him in such a high-pitched shrill that it sounded as though a thousand mosquitoes were swarming the house. I was frightened beyond anything I had known till that day. So frightened I could not intervene and I ran out of the house and down the drive, crying. It took Gryphon an hour to make me smile and only then by showing me that Mr. Douglas was fine. I had never felt such rage before. I had no idea.

I feel a rising sense of panic. Having Kat here has only made it worse, and I wanted her here, I helped her find a hotel, wanted her here like a second sister – one who understands me. Like Norman Douglas, I am trapped. She can leave whenever she wants, though the pull of Papa Freud is hard to resist. She is not a miserable wretch, scared off easily. Now I wish she were.

Ernst and I decide to talk to Klara about our

mother. Like Lucie's mother, she is ignoring the whole situation. She goes to her friends or they come to our house, and I bake them tarts made of sweet dough and filled with almond paste. I scrape off the darkest patches from the burnt bottoms before I serve them. They sit in the living room balancing their coffee cups on their knees and discussing their children, recent weddings, funerals, and books as if the world is an orderly place. Before they come over, my mother asks me to bundle all the newspapers Ernst takes and throw them away. She wants no reminders of "that business." My mother has a bosom, as Klara would call it, and she dresses her bosom in pearls when her friends come. She wears clothes that have been kept clean in the closet in paper, and she shines her shoes. I have to shine the silver, as we have no maid anymore. Her friends must notice that it's Alice, the one who's distracted and jumpy, serving the coffee, but they are too kind to mention it.

Sitting in the kitchen crushing the burnt bottoms of the tarts I cut off between our fingers, Ernst and I decide it is time to talk to Klara. Mother listens to Klara so we hope she can help us get through to mother that the world is falling apart.

"Albatross," Ernst says. He has a few nicknames for me, and this is my least favorite. "What are we going to tell her anyway, 'Sorry mother, the world of your childhood is no more. Accept it?'"

"How about, 'Wise up and get out.'" I say.

"Oh, that's useful. Good one. Where would we go anyhow?"

"Who cares. Far away from here and from the kaffeeklatch," I point out the kitchen door.

"I am much more worried about Hitler than the ladies in the other room, Schmalice."

"Because they are not worried that you will be an old maid."

"No, they are trying to interest me in their daughters, fat and thin."

"Sorry, you poor good catch."

He is a good catch – thin, dark, tall with strong eyebrows and curly hair that he tames with oil, but parts of it flop into his eyes when he is reading. He will be a good father someday – one with humor and the ability to love – if he escapes my mother.

After the women leave, I go to Klara's bookshop and follow her around as she wraps books in brown paper and string for her customers to carry home. She has on a thick white apron, and her hair is tucked behind her ears so earnestly I am afraid to confront her. She is twitchy and her smile is thin, her lips tight. I don't have to tell her that I am scared – she shares a bed with me. I try to convince her that we should be talking to our mother about what is going on.

"To what end, Alice?"

"Ernst and I think she is fooling herself."

"What's it to you if she is?"

"We think she should be aware."

"Of what? That we have political difficulties? That this might be the newest pogrom? That we are impoverished and so is everyone else? Oh Alice, you are so childish. Let her live her life any way she wants. Nothing she does will make any difference."

"Klara, our lives are in danger."

"Alice, you love a crisis. That way you can escape with good reason."

"Klara, this is not personal."

"How do you know? To you, everything is personal."

I want to wring her neck. Not because I am afraid of the Nazis, but because she is the good daughter and I am the bad one who everyone talks about until I walk in the room and then they are silent. What have I ever done to arouse such concern?

I look around the shop with its walls of books and the ladders that roll to reach the top shelves and the U-shaped desk in the middle where Klara takes money and wraps books. It is gleaming, no dust anywhere, not even on the top shelves. The fittings on the ladders are shining, the front window with its display of books stacked neatly to show their spines has no fingerprints or smudges. Everything looks perfect. Klara smiles and walks towards a new customer. Her back looks like mine must to someone else. Erect, thin, tiny, so easily snapped in two. I want to wrap her in brown paper and put her on a high shelf where no one will hurt her, she and my mother, like two pink-cheeked china dolls.

Excerpt from a letter from Bryher to H.D.
Villa Kenwin
March 25, 1933

"Alice alone in the mountains sounds most alarming for her companion: poor old gentleman."

Chapter 13

Klara thinks I need to take some air. I wonder if she is trying to get me away from mother so I don't disturb the equilibrium Klara works to preserve. I see no point in letting mother be a child. I want to get out of Vienna. There is no walking at night any more, no strolling down the street to the Opera. There are too many soldiers and protesters in the streets, too much fear of violence. I can't see Victor because I can't go to the café alone. What would Ernst say if I asked him to come meet my secret *goyische* lover so that we can make cow eyes at each other in the front window of Café Central?

There is only looking over your shoulder now. Wondering, will the Germans come? At least that is what Gryphon believes. Will the war start today? Will it start before Kat can go? Will she be stuck here? Gryphon writes in code, sending messages from Vevey, from London, from America, with news of what forces build and dissipate.

Dr. J thinks I am heated, my fantasies grown out of proportion to my life. He is worried that my desire for Victor is an escape from some earlier trauma, and also an escape from the mounting uncertainties here. Somehow it is also an unhealthy identification with Gryphon. He wants me to go where I cannot feel either. He wants me to give Victor up and thinks if he sends me away, I will have to. And then I can complete my treatment.

I should go, walk, use my body. But I only want one thing, to be in Victor's arms the way I have seen lovers be, the way I dream of. Is that too much to hope for? That I could be one of those people locked in an embrace?

In reality, I am tricking everyone. It eats at my conscience terribly. Klara is such a sweet girl, the way a Viennese girl should be. In the way I pretend to be. I simply do what she does. Do what I imagine sweet Klara would do in her bookstore with her lady customers buying cookery books to be better hostesses. Look at the ground when I walk. Talk softly. Never look anyone in the eye. I can see it frightens Kat to see me here.

And I am about to fool sweet Klara into something that will ruin me in her eyes if she ever finds out.

Victor is going to take some air himself. His swim club is going to compete in the mountains against some team or another, or so Lucie tells me as we sit in her room and plan. Lucie's team is going too, and she will invite me to come see her compete. For all we know, it will be the last time Hakoach will leave Vienna to compete anywhere. We will be terribly well-supervised by her coach, who chases everyone around, making sure we are all in our rooms after dinner, and only girls with girls and boys with boys. But once he is gone, he doesn't come back. I will be in the same hotel as Victor. Lucie is going to give me the money to rent my own room and not share hers. Maybe I can beg some seductive clothes from Kat.

Victor is taken aback by the gesture. Bemused and intrigued. Frightened. I can see that he is frightened by the way his shoulders squeeze forward and pinch his ears. They get wider in the back and narrower in the front when I tell him my plan.

I am demure, and look away, like I have seen the actress Elisabeth Bergner do in Ibsen plays. When she is looking like a woman should, helpless. Then she turns and plays a man in a suit in the next movie. Perhaps he has not seen that movie. Perhaps all the time at the University and in the coffeehouses has helped him stay so delicate and smooth. Am I ruining him too?

Chapter 14

Traveling between Vienna and the mountains, I am floating along on the surface. Skimming as a rock does across the surface of the water. Jumping once, twice, three times if thrown right, before sinking into the lake, below the reflection of the trees and the clouds, into the heart of the lake, the heart of things. Into what really matters.

On the train, I spread out my lunch and eat the bread and cheese and drink the beer that Klara packed for me, warm and fizzy from the motion of the car against the rail. I am not home and I am not in myself either.

The family across from me sees a Jewish girl traveling alone. I may not look Jewish to Kat in Vevey, but on a train in Austria I may as well wear a sign that says "Jew." They ignore me and talk amongst themselves, which is fine with me. My mind wanders so that I only smile absently at the blondish-grey woman, at her husband who talks so knowingly and loudly about each subject and is wrong about everything, and nod at their country speech.

In my mind, I am almost in the hotel, almost in Victor's arms. I am in the future, as one always is on a trip. Travel to a place always takes longer than the trip back, perhaps because you are living in the arrival. Living to return is a reluctant trip, but somehow faster for the reluctance.

I wonder what it will be like to be lovers. To have a lover as Kat has lovers. Not a schoolgirl crush or whatever I have had before. I am not a girl anymore. I am a woman, or waiting to be a woman.

When I traveled with Pup and Kat all around Europe, I was free to have crushes. I bored Kat with them, tormented her with the meetings and the departures of love and affection. The lazily placed finger that may or may not have been on purpose. The lingering good-byes at train stations and docks with boys I would forget instantly.

I know she thinks this is one of those crushes. One of those accidental meetings where I am making more of it in my mind than it is in his heart.

I find the hotel. I find my room. I feel hungry and no one is there to tell me it is time to eat, or not. Hakoach is practicing in a natatorium somewhere. I am free to do exactly as I choose. I pick up the heavy-curved silver in the dining room at exactly the time I see fit. I eat what I choose off the menu and promptly forget about it. I walk around the square in my sweater by myself, and I enter the world of women. I have made my first moment of adult life. Not by making love, which I thought would define me as a woman. By making the thousand choices no one ever lets me make in my day. Not even in Vevey, where I was subject to Pup's schedule. Here, I am only for myself.

I lie across the bed in my room thinking of Victor, with my hands wandering my body, in and out of my depths. I have taken off my stockings, my shoes, taken my hair out of the pins that hold it back, and I am on the bed I will sleep in, alone.

I am free to touch myself as Victor would, with no fear of waking Klara. I can litter the bed with my books, mostly texts by Papa Freud, no novels or histories, but that is romantic enough for me. I can sleep this way, having pleasured myself, can fall asleep with the lights on, with no one to bother and no one to consult about safety or the bedcovers, no child to check on, no sister in the bed. I am an adult for the first time in my life.

Tomorrow will be another day much like today except Victor will be in it. Victor, and if I manage to avoid Hakoach and the swimmers, almost no one else in this most unseasonable early spring trip.

I meet Victor at breakfast and he is thrilled and a bit aghast to see me.

"Alice," he says, "Alice, I am so surprised to see you."

As if it is our private jest. As if we are pretending we ran into each other by accident.

We walk in and out of the edges of the forest around the town. He is scared to go in too deep. It gets so dense so quickly, the branches intertwined and the light stolen from the ground. The ground has thawed in patches, but at the edge of the forest there is snow and mud and trees so thick that we could never weave through. I remember Kat's description of how quickly the forest swallows you up.

Better, I guess, that we stay where it is safe, where we can see the town.

But the deeper forest is exciting. Parts would be so deep that the ground would be dry, the evergreens keeping the snow from reaching the floor. Scented from the needles of the trees, we could have made an aromatic nest and stayed forever.

Instead, we go back to the hotel, Victor to meet his team and me to bathe for him. I take extra caution to clean with scented soap. It smells like adulthood to me, like lavender scented maturity. I wash between my legs, under my arms, up my neck, under my breasts, all the places Victor will need. The washcloth slides so effortlessly between my legs. The soap stings and tingles where I have not been able to keep my fingers out.

To describe making love for the first time is to tell where hands go. Where the mouths meet and where the noses must move to gracefully avoid one another. It is an endless series of intricate gestures that leads one deeper into the maze – the minotaur's labyrinth – so that in the middle, one is met by the half-man, half-bull beast of one's desire. Then, like in the myth, I disappear. Ravished, I disappear from my own view.

Not saved by the gods, but completely abandoned by them and by everything I understand. I can only touch him, run my fingers over the soft hair on his chest, feel his arms where they curve with muscle, touch his sides and his legs. I am mesmerized by his body; how it forms a pyramid shape with ridges of muscle and soft hair that is so light and so straight. All of my hair, everywhere, is so curly. I want to bite his tongue when he puts it in my mouth. I do nibble his lips as I am kissing them, just enough to make him make a noise. What I enjoy most is how ardently he touches me, how careful he is not to miss an inch of my skin as he moves his hands over me. He is reluctant at first to go anywhere interesting, as though he cannot believe his good fortune and does not want to risk it. He will approach my breasts and veer off to my stomach. I wiggle so that he has to touch them and then he cannot leave them alone, kissing, stroking. He takes my nipple between his teeth and I feel stars move down my spine. Eventually I need to take his hand and put it on me where he won't. He lets out a low noise and I whisper to him, *"J'ai envie."* How gentle he is, and how unsure of where to put his fingers, but this I do know and so I show him.

I saw Ernst bathing when we were children, and it did not look like this. There is skin where Ernst had none, and I would have known this if I'd thought of it, or talked to Lucie, but I didn't. I am fascinated. I slide down so that I can take it in my hands and touch it. Run my fingers lightly over the outside as Victor relaxes into the bed. I hold onto it, but don't have much idea what to do. Victor reaches over my hand and shows me how to move, so that I am pretending he is making love to my hand. I lean in and lick the tip as my hand is moving, and he likes that. I lick further down, letting my tongue touch his foreskin. I wiggle the tip of my tongue under it and lick around the head and I forget for a moment there is a person on the other end, the smell, the taste of him drawing me in. He is still there with a look of surprise and happiness on his face. Lucie is right. I have been wasting my life.

The first moments of trying to fit together

are funny, but Victor doesn't think so. I can tell he is embarrassed by what he doesn't know, and I am momentarily frightened it will hurt. It is supposed to, but with all the time I have spent with my fingers inside me, it really isn't that painful. He is over me, looking down at me with my hair spilling over the pillow and I am looking at him. We form one person. I want to try everything I can think of. I sit astride him, I let him put my legs where he wants, I feel my passion for him grow as we move legs and disconnect to reconnect some other way. Victor, behind me, holding fast to my hips with one hand, and with his other hand touching me as I have only touched myself. I cannot see him, but I feel him moving inside me. I start to slip away. I know what the *petit mort* is like when I am alone. This is not that death at all. It is as though I cannot tell his hand from my body, nor can I feel where what is inside of me leaves off, and becomes him. When I can no longer hold on I shudder in his hands and I slip out from his grasp.

He dresses to go to the bathroom in the hall and I cannot ask him not to go. His leaving is wrong to me. It has a feeling of cowardice to it, of not being willing to follow your heart through to the other side. When you truly care about your heart, you don't get swayed by how things look. I know that from Gryphon. This is not a popular belief; Papa Freud and Dr. Jekels will have much to say about it.

To imagine that they do this every night, in their own beds with their wives, is astounding. That the world of married people, the world of lovers, has this secret life all its own, that they can access this all the time. Can it be that this feeling is shared by other people, or did we, in the special power of our passion, create something extraordinary that no one else has made? I want to believe that Victor could never do that with anyone else and neither can I. I know this is not true and it deflates me.

He returns to say good night and kisses me on the nose. I shudder with unmistakable re-vulsion, which he mistakes for passion. He goes to sleep in his own room.

Chapter 15

Lucie and I are walking down the street, away from the hotel, to give us a chance to talk about my night. Szigo, her coach, has been chasing everyone around the town making sure there are no rendezvous. He has promised parents their girls are safe. How anyone could be safe around water polo players in tiny white bathing suits with a blue stripe accenting just the right place, is probably not what parents need to hear. We just want five minutes to talk and only plan to walk around the block. As I am getting to the part where I see him naked for the first time, Lucie stops. She points down the street where a group of boys from Ewask are surrounding Fritzi, a boy from the Hakoach water polo team. They are shouting at him, "No Jews or Dogs allowed in the Park" and laughing. This, we have heard, is the sign posted in Germany. Fritzi is completely calm, even though there are ten of them to one of him. I panic and want to run and get help. I am not sure who I will get. The police don't care, and we have snuck away from Szigo, so he's not a good option. I think of Victor, but these are his teammates. I am so scared that I start to shake. Lucie, who is fearless to a fault, begins to walk over to the boys.

Once, when Lucie and I were about twelve, we took Klara on a bobsled ride. We were warned at the top not to head straight down the hill, that we would not be able to stop at the bottom, that it was dangerous. Lucie was steering and she did not just head straight down, she steered into the fall line so we went down faster and faster with each curve, gaining speed until we reached the bottom and, as warned, could not stop. We flew through a crowd of people, and collided with a tree. Lucie, who was in front, broke her arm. I was bruised up and down my back from where I fell. Klara went home crying, and Lucie had to be talked into seeing a doctor before she took the sled up one more time. Her Papa says he is afraid of her because she does not know fear. Klara still avoids Lucie because she is not interested in being frightened to death.

I see Fritzi in the middle of the street and his eyes have a familiar look. He is standing tall, chin up, arms loosely at his side, for all the world a brave boy. That look is what I saw in the mirror last night as I cleaned my teeth — eyes shifting, looking for a place to land, finding nothing familiar. I am not Lucie, and I do fear for my limbs, but not at the expense of my heart or I would not be here at all.

I run up to Lucie and we link arms. We smile and pat the boys on the shoulder and then duck between them to get to Fritzi.

"Come along Fritzi darling, let's go, this is no place for us," Lucy purrs.

"Yes, Fritzi, we have things to do," I add, and turn to face the crowd.

Lucie begins to walk back through the boys, holding Fritzi's arm, and she smiles at the boys and says, "Excuse me," as she steps on one boy's foot. The boys are so surprised to see us walking right past them as if we are not afraid, that they just let Fritzi go. When we have walked a slow, sweaty few paces away from them, we start to run. We have a lead of about ten paces and Lucie and Fritzi are in good athletic form. They begin to sprint and I can't quite keep up. I look back and the Ewask boys are following me, not at a full run, but contemplating if they should try to catch me once I am alone.

As we are running, and I am slowing down, I pass Victor. He is on the other side of the street, which is narrow. I am so relieved to see him I slow down to a walk and begin to cross to his side of the street, aware of the footfalls now gaining on me. Victor looks at me, at the boys behind me, and he keeps walking. He averts his gaze, as though not looking at me means I cannot see him. I do see him, and I see all our futures in him.

I stop and turn around to watch him as he passes the Ewask boys. His green wool coat familiar, the lapels fraying. The back of his head held high, and frozen. The glass wall in Café Central is nothing compared to what I feel here on the street in the cold air of the Alps. He is willing, after I have tasted the core of him, to pass me by and not stop. We are doomed. Not the Jews, not women, but our age is doomed to what Gryphon has seen coming.

Those meetings will never end the war, there

will be no real fight over Austria. I know in that moment that people will cheer in the streets when Hitler marches into the country. They will embrace someone on whom to project their deepest desires. That is all he is, someone to act out their most gnarled fantasies.

The Ewask boys give Victor a wave of recognition. With his blonde hair and his broad shoulders he looks like a poster boy for the master race. While he is going to meetings and spending time with me, he is also swimming on a team that only allows Aryans. He may be against the Nazis but not exactly for the Jews either. Papa Altshul says ninety-five percent of Austria would be glad to see us gone. If Victor wants to protect Austria from the North, it must be for other reasons than saving me. If Victor wants to play in the dark, it is also for other reasons than saving me.

I turn and take off to catch up with Lucie and Fritzi. We run all the way to the hotel and into the dining room where there are a few girls sitting playing cards. We are crying, and laughing, and hugging them and they don't know why. But we do. It is good, in the face of such danger and fear, to feel you belong some-where and have friends.

I go pack my things and move them to Lucie's room. There are now four girls in two beds with one shared bathroom in the hall, but I am happy. I cuddle up next to Lucie after we turn the lights off and I smell her hair. She smells like not quite dry towels and pool water. The room is silent but for the breathing of the other girls. The dark has a warm, brown velvet quality. There are all sorts of heroism and all sorts of evil, and it is very easy to tell the difference between the two.

Excerpt of a letter, H.D. to Bryher
Hotel Regina, Vienna
April 27, 1933

"Yes, do, do have A. at once. She is a menace
to Vienna, tugging at the lead. . ."

Chapter 16

The streets are empty of all but papers floating up from the ground. Propaganda. I will not read them. The fascists, the Nazis, all the same to me; politics mean nothing since I have no one to discuss it with but Kat. Victor is not around these days to explain his views. I have not seen him at Café Central, have not heard from him, and I have not gone looking. Why look for trouble, it's on its way soon enough. This I cannot discuss either, except with Lucie, who is so cavalier. "Who cares," she says. "Who cares, you are alive, you loved it." I realize that no one saw what I saw – Lucie had been focused on Fritzi and Fritzi would not know Victor from any other man on the street. I never need to tell anyone how one day I opened myself and let him slip inside, taking pleasure in gulps, and how the next he cut me dead on the street when the violence was already happening. Even Victor may have been wise enough to know that there was nothing to sustain, and no way to keep this going. We could never, and yet we did, and now I have to live with the space Victor occupied.

I am worried about all the papers floating around. I am worried that we are missing the message as we step over them to walk to ps-a. Dr. Jekels doesn't care for them, nor does he want to discuss my interest in how all this propaganda could be floating around and yet we could still have no real idea what is going on. He wants to know about my trip. I tell him the mountains were very beautiful. I tell him the train trip felt freeing. I tell him Vienna feels restrictive. When he probes for detail, I realize I will never be Kat, open to ps-a, open to the world through words. I just want to keep what is secret away from the spotlight of his intellect. I realize this analysis is not working. Dr. Jekels is doing his part, but I am not doing mine. Right now I don't want an unrestricted view of my unconscious, I just want to be able to see the paving stones emerge from under the papers as if from snowmelt. I am even keeping the information about Victor from him, as he would only look smug and say the psychoanalytic equivalent of "I told you so."

I do tell him that a friend of Klara's jumped from a building yesterday. A very stable and friendly girl, who was engaged to be married, and who displayed every bit of the demeanor Dr. Jekels wants for me.

"They found a note on her desk that described how she felt about ending her life, 'If not for the coming war, this would be difficult.'"

When I leave Dr. Jekels, I realize I will need to tell Kat I am a failed analysand. Hopefully I can keep from spilling the rest. When I arrive she is in her dressing gown, hair not brushed, letters spread around her on the bed and clothes in piles on the floor. She is talking fast, in her mode of agitation and worry. I forget about Dr. Jekels, my infirmities, even about Victor.

"Alice, would you like to go to Vevey and meet Pup when she returns from Greece?"

I am speechless, and nod. As if she needed to ask.

"I have been given twelve weeks with Dr. Freud, and I am going to stay to finish them, but when I am done, I will meet you there. You need to make sure Gryphon knows I am safe."

"That would be a lie."

"Maybe so, but I will finish and come home safely, I promise you. And you must promise her. And bring her this soap," she gestures to twelve bars of soap on the bed.

I must look confused because Kat laughs at me, as if everyone ships soap to Switzerland from Vienna with a Jewish courier before Hitler invades and the economy collapses.

"The clothes in those piles are for you and for Klara, divide them up. Tell your mother I will come over and explain all the details as soon as I get dressed."

Kat and Gryphon seem to believe that the threat from the North continues to wax daily, and so I am running manically around the bedroom throwing clothes in a satchel, trying to figure out what the weather will be like in Vevey and how long I will be there and how long they will keep me once Pup comes back from her European tour.

Klara wants the silver silk scarf and I let her take it. She also thinks we should give the coat I love so much, the one that is almost shiny and made from what looks like satin, to these twins we know who are sharing one coat between the two of them.

"They are too fat," I tell her, and I put the coat on in front of the mirror. It is a little too big for me but I try to fill it out to make my point. Klara is not fooled. She is used to cutting down Kat's clothes to fit me.

"They are sharing a coat, you ungrateful child. They can't even go out at the same time. They have to take turns."

I pull the coat around me tighter. I know I will have to give it up later, but I want to wear it for a while.

Of course there were things about Villa Kenwin I did not like. I have to relax and wait for them to come back to me, now that I know I am going back. I don't mind the Quex, the Dragon housekeeper who used to make me crazy. I can fight any dragon in the kitchen now. She was my nemesis, and so Kat named her the Dragon. She would wait in the dark in the kitchen to pounce on me if I went in for hot milk in the middle of the night. She guarded the kitchen with her evil drunken eye and flirted with the male visitors. What a grotesque thought, this old woman drunk and inappropriately throwing herself at Norman Douglas or some other writer who came into the kitchen expecting a piece of bread for indigestion after dinner. She had the sense that she was being ignored, her natural beauty passed over for Kat, and she was jealous. Always looking for a way to punish all of us. But compared to life here, she is a boon.

I will have my room back at the end of the hall, the room that connects to Pup's and from that perch I can watch the rest of them. I can watch over Pup with hawk eyes, even if she is no longer a little girl. I can watch out for Kat much more easily there. If I could just get this pink chemise into this bag.

Gryphon promises that when she helps Papa Freud, Ernst, and the others leave, she will get my mother and Klara to leave, too. They are as stupid and complacent as the cows I saw from the train window coming home from the mountains. No matter how dire the situation, the antimacassars are straightened and the fire is lit, and everything is just fine. Well, if Gryphon can work the miracle of convincing Mama that I can leave her once again, when

I thought I would smother under the eider-down in my sleep, then I believe that when she thinks it is no longer safe for the Jews, she will be able to move that herd of cows out too.

In the meantime, I am free of them. No more Klara and her perfect hems. No more burnt bottoms on the buns I was supposed to gently heat. Only a good-bye session with Dr. Jekels and farewells to my family. I see how they stare at me out of the corners of their eyes, poor Alice will never be a real woman, she is too wild. I may never find the stolid center they want, but I am going back to a place that demands something altogether different from me. Something the world could use these days.

Chapter 17

n my last visit with Dr. Jekels before I go, I want to explain it all to him so he understands. If I am leaving, there is no reason to keep my own counsel. I no longer see the purpose in dissimulation. Maybe it is a breakthrough, the one Kat was waiting for, but he just listens as usual.

"Victor was standing there," I tell him. "Just on the same street, he didn't even stop to do anything. If he did not stop and help me, who in the entire world would? Kat and Gryphon would. They have not only stopped on the street and extended a hand, but they have promised to save my family, you, Dr. Freud, his family, and anyone else they can."

He nods. He is silent, the perfect screen for my need to understand what happened. Why did I not see him this way all along?

"Don't you see, that bond, that sacred bond of lovers, I thought when I saw other people emerge from it that they were altered. They were improved. They were blessed by Aphrodite. Maybe she is fickle, and inconstant, but she does bewitch people for a while. I thought I would be bewitched too. I thought I would be made whole. I thought by feeling the texture of him, I would change. Maybe at some other time, maybe if the world were different."

"Alice," Dr. Jekels says to me in his heavy Viennese accent, so different from the Swiss German I would be hearing soon, so different from Kat's schoolgirl German. "Alice, it does not happen that way. You create it here on this couch in this room by piecing together the lost artifacts of your soul."

Dr. Jekels is an old man. He has lived through the Great War. He lived in Vienna with Wittgenstein, Schoenberg. He has a wife, children, grandchildren. He must see life coiled out behind him, a spider's sticky tensile web of associations, images, dreams, desires, fetishes, overdetermination, and moments of clarity. He has found a way to make the story make sense. The past you build from, associate with; the future you assure by the time you spend in this room. I want to believe it is like this, believe what Kat and Gryphon do, that ps-a will save me, that telling the story will save me, but in the tension behind my throat there is not room to swallow even psychoanalysis.

I tell him one last dream, hoping it will make sense. I tell him the dream where I am in the river, under the crystal clear water. I can see it flow over me only by texture. I am at the bottom, motionless. The clouds are moving in the sky above me, and I can see them through the ripples of the water. Divers are coming in, slicing the water with their bodies, making a trail of bubbles as they silently pass me, not moving the water around me, but close enough that I can see their features. Lucie goes by, as does Victor, and Ernst. They are naked, newborn to the water, and sleek. Outside the water I see my mother and Klara on the bank, surrounded by milling people, agitated and pressing toward the edge. Some move as if to dive but do not, some turn their backs on the water and walk heavy-footed away from the bank. They are lost to my sight in a few steps. There are no water maidens swimming past, and I know the Narns have gone. That the rope has been severed. The Narns have made their cut.

The gods Kat and Gryphon write about and worship are also gone. Their hall on Olympus is empty, dust blows through in eddies. But I cannot see where the swimmers have gone, they are past me and out of sight. The water is growing cold. Faint voices reach me from ahead and they pull me slowly like a current. I want to go that way, but the people on the bank pull me in the other direction with their sharp gestures and their dark clothing. They feel heavy, they feel solid, they have a gravitational pull. The current is moving me before I have a chance to decide. It pulls me and I float effortlessly into the sunlight. Then I wake up.

"What do you think?" Dr. Jekels asks me. He nods and smiles at me; he knows what he wants me to say and I have made him happy with this dream. He is once again the sweet trickster jaguar god of the deep water, and I want to say something profound that will be an offering to him, will appease him and make my passage a safe one. What I tell him I know I will remember always. Not because it is perfect, or because I had the wisdom then to know what he was asking of me, but because it is simply true. It is true despite how little I did know, and it will be borne out by the events that follow.

At that moment how could I have known that the Great War would not be the end to wars, that a Second World War would begin and Vienna would be swallowed up? I did not yet know I would travel from Vevey with Kat once the war started, starved and frightened, my Austrian passport hidden in my suitcase, as far as the hot, dirty port in Spain only to be turned back. Or that eventually Gryphon would find us and get us to England. That we would leave Vevey with every other expatriate resident and never see a single one again. That I would live out my life speaking English and walking in Hyde Park, thinking of those linden trees and feeling my mind drawn back to them again and again. But, that was years in the future and all I knew when I was talking to Dr. J was how to leave.

"Alice, do you know how to get to the bank on the other side of your dream, the one you cannot see?"

I say to him: "The past is only what we choose to cling to, no matter how heavy it feels in our hands. The future glides ahead of us, and we have no way to it yet. I simply let go. I simply let go again and again and do not resist the current. What will happen, even the gods don't know."

Acknowledgements

This book would not have happened without Felix Wittern helping me with my German and with research on Jewish life in Vienna. I am indebted to Dan Sargent for his obsession with H.D. and *The H.D. Book* before it existed in print, and to Steven Taylor for letting me write about H.D. theoretically.

Alice Modern was a real person. She is mentioned exactly eight times, seven in the letters between H.D. and Winifred Bryher, and one other time in a journal from one of their friends. So, that much is true. Every possible other thing is fiction. Ergo, anything that is incorrect, anachronistic, or just plain wrong is mine. Much of the research on H.D. came from her own writing and her letters with Bryher, as well as from Robert Duncan's *The H.D. Book*.

Andrew Wille is an extraordinary reader and editor who saw the shape of the book before it was done. Laurie Mitchell had her hand in this, as with all my books, and made sure there was no messiness. Thank you to Laird Hunt for his input and to Tak Kendrick, Mike Barber, Jon Nystrom, Marilyn Talmage, Nat Coakley, Alexandra Hidalgo, and Tom Henwood for the weekly critique that kept me honest.

Safia Radha Ohlson knows everything about everything that is worth anything – writing or otherwise.

Jerry Kelly and Jenaye Hill are my heroes for taking Alice on, as is Jason Anthony for representing her and me. My appreciation to Kaitlin Tebeau for her sharp eye and edits.

And, to Allan Cole for asking the question: "Did you write about redemption?" Yes I did, AC, and I always do.

Always, always my deepest gratitude is for my children: Zach, Emma, and Zoë.

Michelle Auerbach is the author of The Third Kind of Horse (2013, Beatdom Books). Her writing has appeared in The New York Times and the literary anthologies The Veil (UC Berkley Press), Uncontained (Baksun Books), and You: An Anthology of Essays in the Second Person (Welcome Table Press). Michelle is the winner of the 2011 Northern Colorado Fiction Prize. This is her second novel.